W9-BPL-806

A Note to Parents

Reading books aloud and playing word games are two valuable ways parents can help their children learn to read. The easy-to-read stories in the **My First Hello Reader! With Flash Cards** series are designed to be enjoyed together. Six activity pages and 16 flash cards in each book help reinforce phonics, sight vocabulary, reading comprehension, and facility with language. Here are some ideas to develop your youngster's reading skills:

Reading with Your Child

- Read the story aloud to your child and look at the colorful illustrations together. Talk about the characters, setting, action, and descriptions. Help your child link the story to events in his or her own life.
- Read parts of the story and invite your child to fill in the missing parts. At first, pause to let your child "read" important last words in a line. Gradually, let your child supply more and more words or phrases. Then take turns reading every other line until your child can read the book independently.

Enjoying the Activity Pages

- Treat each activity as a game to be played for fun. Allow plenty of time to play.
- Read the introductory information aloud and make sure your child understands the directions.

Using the Flash Cards

- Read the words aloud with your child. Talk about the letters and sounds and meanings.
- Match the words on the flash cards with the words in the story.
- Help your child find words that begin with the same letter and sound, words that rhyme, and words with the same ending sound.
- Challenge your child to put flash cards together to make sentences from the story and create new sentences.

Above all else, make reading time together a fun time. Show your child that reading is a pleasant and meaningful activity. Be generous with your praise and know that, as your child's first and most important teacher, you are contributing immensely to his or her command of the printed word.

—Tina Thoburn, Ed.D.
Educational Consultant

Copyright © 1997 by Nancy Hall, Inc.
All rights reserved. Published by Scholastic Inc.
MY FIRST HELLO READER!, CARTWHEEL BOOKS, and the
CARTWHEEL BOOKS logo are registered trademarks of Scholastic Inc.
The MY FIRST HELLO READER! logo is a trademark of Scholastic Inc.

Library of Congress Cataloging-in-Publication Data
Packard, Mary.
    I am not a dinosaur / by Mary Packard; illustrated by Nate Evans.
        p.   cm. — (My first hello reader!)
    "Cartwheel books."
    "With flash cards."
    "Preschool - grade 1" — Cover.
    Summary: A baby rhamphorynchus envies the dinosaurs which have horns, roars, legs, and other characteristics, but finally decides that he's quite happy with his flying wings.
    ISBN 0-590-68997-5
    [1. Pterosaurs — Fiction. 2. Prehistoric animals — Fiction. 3. Stories in rhyme.]
    I. Evans, Nate, ill. II. Title. III. Series.
PZ8.3.P125Iad   1997
[E] — dc20   96-75
                                                                     CIP
                                                                     AC
1 2 3 4 5 6/0   20 19 18 17 16 15 14 13

Printed in the U.S.A.   23

First Scholastic printing, February 1997

I AM NOT A DINOSAUR

by Mary Packard
Illustrated by Nate Evans

My First Hello Reader!
With Flash Cards

SCHOLASTIC INC.

New York   Toronto   London   Auckland   Sydney

I am not a dinosaur.

I don't have horns.

My legs are short.

My feet are small—

Not like a dinosaur at all!

I wish I had a special tail,

A longer neck,

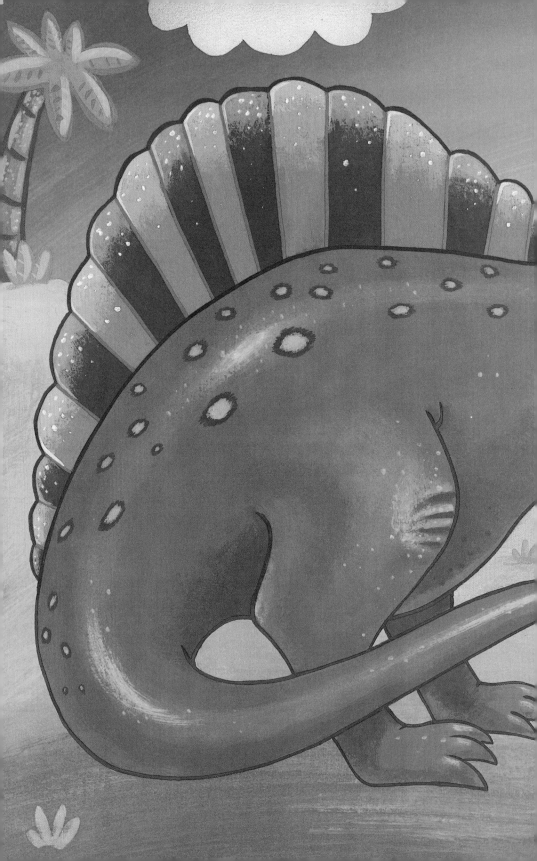

A special sail.

Although I do not have a crest,

I do have wings!

Wings are the best!

Fly Away

The animal in this story is not a dinosaur.
It is a **Rhamphorynchus**!
It has wings and can fly, and is actually a bird.

If you had wings like the **Rhamphorynchus**,
where would *you* fly?

Dinosaur Search

Find five dinosaurs hidden in this picture.

D Is for Dinosaurs

Point to the pictures of the words that begin with the letter D.

Rhyming Words

In each row, point to the object that rhymes with the word on the left.

tail

crest

horn

wing

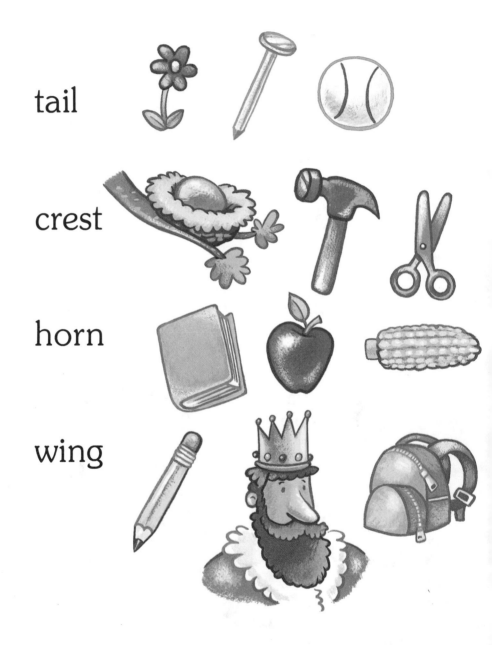

Words and Meanings

Some words have more than one meaning.

A **horn** is a part of an animal,
and a **horn** is also a musical instrument.

The first sentence in each pair gives one meaning
for a word. Read the second sentence and point to
the picture at the bottom of the page that shows
another meaning of that word.

A **ring** is a sound that a telephone makes.
A **ring** is also a

A **ball** is a fancy party where people dance.
A **ball** is also a

A **pen** is a place where pigs are kept.
A **pen** is also a

Animals

Some animals have body parts that make them different from other animals.

Match each animal on the left to its special body part on the right.

bull

fin

fish

wing

bird

shell

turtle

horn

Answers

(Fly Away)

Answers will vary.

(Dinosaur Search)

The hidden dinosaurs
are circled here ------------>

(D is for Dinosaurs)

These begin with D:

(Rhyming Words)

| tail | crest | horn | wing |

(Words and Meanings)

A ring is also a

A ball is also a

A pen is also a

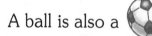

(Animals)

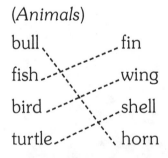

bull — fin
fish — wing
bird — shell
turtle — horn